About the

Emily's first book, *Astrid the Au Pair from Outer Space*, won the prestigious Smarties Silver Award. 'It was totally unexpected,' says Emily. 'I was so taken aback I even forgot to grab the free Smarties.'

She has always been interested in jokes, particularly bad ones. 'Though I'm no good at telling jokes,' she says. 'When I try at home, the usual response is, "Oh, do shut up, Mum."' So that is why, like Ed in *What Howls at the Moon in Frilly Knickers*, she has to laugh at her own jokes.

Emily was born in London, and now lives in Oxfordshire. She has no hobbies. Or frilly knickers.

For my mother

ORCHARD BOOKS
96 Leonard Street, London EC2A 4XD
Orchard Books Australia
Unit 31/56 O'Riordan Street, Alexandria, NSW 2015
A PAPERBACK ORIGINAL
First published in Great Britain in 2001
Text © Emily Smith 2001
The right of Emily Smith to be identified as the author has
been asserted by her in accordance with the Copyright, Designs
and Patents Act, 1988.
A CIP catalogue record for this book is available from
the British Library.
ISBN 1 84121 808 1
3 5 7 9 10 8 6 4 2
Printed in Great Britain

What Howls at the Moon in Frilly Knickers?

e. f. smith

ORCHARD BOOKS

Chapter One

There was an old man of Peru,
Whose limericks stopped at line two.

We did the joke book together.

Ed, Gary and me.

But it was my idea.

I think I just wanted to do something – anything – because of Mim. Because I was so cut up about her being ill. You might think that writing a joke book is rather an odd thing to do when your grandmother is…well, dying. Well, you go ahead and think what you like.

It's what I did.

Or rather what we did.

Ed, Gary and me.

But it was my idea.

'*Why do cows have bells?*' said Gary. It was breaktime, and as usual, we were just mooning about.

There was silence.

Then Ed said, 'It's because of the grass.'

Gary looked at him. 'The *grass?*'

'Yes, the grass. How good it is.'

'*What?*'

'If the grass is poor quality, like up a mountain, the cows need a bigger area to graze,' explained Ed happily. 'But they get lost, so farmers put bells on them.'

'Yeah,' said Gary slowly. 'Yeah. That's one way to kill a joke.'

Ed's face fell. 'It was a *joke?*'

'It *was.*'

'Oh,' said Ed.

'So what's the answer, then?' I said.

Gary sighed. '*Because their horns don't work.*'

There was another silence.

Gary kicked a crisp packet. 'It's a bit sad,

trying to tell your mates a joke, and getting lectured on grass quality.'

'Sorry,' said Ed.

'Anorak,' muttered Gary under his breath.

But Ed heard. 'Did you know anorak was an Inuit word?' he said, cheerfully.

'Inuit?' said Gary. '*Inuit?*'

I could see Gary was beginning to lose it, so I said, 'Go on, ask us another joke.'

Ed nodded. 'We'll know this time.'

Gary rolled his eyes. 'OK, you saddoes,' said Gary. '*What's brown and turns cartwheels?*'

We had a few guesses. These ranged from clever (Ed) to very clever (Ed) to frankly rude (me).

Finally Gary told us. '*A horse pulling a cart.*'

'Hmm,' I said. 'Not bad.'

'Yes, that's rather an interesting one,' said Ed. 'It shows that the main meaning of cartwheel is no longer a—'

'Ed!' said Gary.

'Yes?' said Ed.

'Shut up!'

'OK,' said Ed.

Gary turned to me. 'You tell one now, Julian.'

I thought. 'Sorry. My mind's a blank.'

'So what's new?' Gary went on. 'Your mind's always a blank.'

'I just can't remember jokes,' I said. 'I have a *problem* with it. You ought to be kind to me.'

'Yeah, yeah, dimwit.' Gary looked at Ed. 'What about you?'

Ed frowned. *'OK. What's got two feet and goes "Quack, quack?"'*

We couldn't think.

'A duck!' he said triumphantly.

'But…' Gary looked exasperated. 'A duck *has* got two feet and goes quack quack.'

'Exactly,' said Ed.

So Gary started to pretend to strangle Ed.

While he was strangling Ed, I got thinking.

'I wish I could remember jokes,' I said.

'Arrrgh!' went Ed.

'Good jokes, that is.'

'Yuuuuurgh!' went Ed.

'I think we should start writing down the best jokes we hear.'

'Eeeeeurgh!' went Ed.

'In fact, I think we ought to write a joke book.'

There was silence.

Gary stopped strangling Ed.

Ed stopped being strangled.

They both looked at me.

'OK.' said Gary.

So that was it.

We were going to write a joke book.

A book of the best jokes we could find.

It was just one of those ideas that took off.

It would take our minds off things at home. (Gary had his problems too.)

And perhaps bring us a few laughs along the way.

It was Gary, of course, who spotted another plus. He saw the pound signs.

'I see pound signs,' he said, as we packed up at the end of school.

'Yes, Gary,' I said kindly.

'I see pound signs,' he repeated. 'With this joke book.'

'Oh!' I said. 'You mean, sell the joke book?'

Gary nodded. 'We're not writing it for nothing – we're going to sell it.' He slapped one hand into the palm of the other. 'And hey, will it *sell*!'

We looked at him.

'I don't know,' said Ed, who thought it was a question.

Gary pushed him in the chest. 'I'm saying it will! It's what people want – jokes!'

'Good jokes,' I agreed.

'I like bad jokes,' said Ed.

'Look, guys!' said Gary. 'I'm telling you – this book is going to be a *seller*!'

We looked at him.

'We can sell to friends. Family. Door to door. Through the Internet.' Gary's voice was rising. 'We'll sell hun—'

'Ssshh!' I said suddenly.

And Gary ssshed.

We looked round the classroom. There were only a few people left. One, the new girl, Rose or something, was looking over at us.

We turned our backs on her, and put our heads together.

'We'd better keep this under wraps for now,' said Gary sternly. 'We don't want anyone nabbing our idea.'

'My idea,' I said.

'OK,' said Ed. 'So where do we go from here?'

'We find 'em,' said Gary. 'We find the jokes!'

'Where?' said Ed. He looked around as if we thought there were jokes lurking somewhere in the classroom.

'You know, joke books and stuff.'

'Joke books?' Ed frowned. 'But can we…take them from other people's books?'

'Why not?'

'Well, it's copying!'

'It's *copying*!' Gary mimicked.

'Yeah!' said Ed.

'Well, tough! How else do we get 'em?'

Ed thought. 'Couldn't we make them up?'

'*Make* them *up*?'

'Yes!'

'Right!' There was a glint in Gary's eye. 'You go home and make some jokes up, Ed. We'll look forward to hearing them tomorrow!'

Chapter Two

Bad spellers of the world untie.

I stuck my head round Mim's door. The gas fire was on. There was a book lying open on the table beside her. But she wasn't reading now. She was sitting in her chair, doing nothing. Just staring. At nothing.

I took a step into the room. 'Mim!' I called softly. (Her real name was Miriam, but I had called her 'Mim' as a toddler – *aaah!* – and it had sort of stuck.)

She looked up – and suddenly her face was alive. 'Julian!' She stretched out her arms. 'Come and give me a kiss.'

I went and put my arms round her, and hugged her thin body, not too tight. 'How's my boy?' she said, as I sat down beside her on the old covered stool. 'Working hard at school, I hope?'

'Sure!' I said.

'Getting on better with maths?'

'Oh, Einstein!' I said.

She gave me a look. 'I seem to remember Einstein *wasn't* very good at maths at school.'

'Ah.' I grinned. 'Hey, maybe that explains it!'

Mim laughed. It turned into a cough, not a bad one. 'So tell me, what homework have you got tonight?'

'Oh, nothing much. Just a bit of English.'

Mim shook her head. 'I reckon they don't work you hard enough. I've a good mind to ring up that head teacher and tell him so.'

'You wouldn't.'

A gleam came into her eye. 'Oh, wouldn't I?'

I decided to change the subject. 'So what are you reading?'

Mim picked the book up – it was a hardback with an old-fashioned cover. 'Something I never read before, but always meant to,' she sighed. 'But I don't seem to be getting it.'

14

My grandmother loved to read. Dad had offered her a telly in her own room, even before she had cancer, but she had said no. Instead she had a floor to ceiling bookcase crammed with books. And she usually had two or three on the go from the library.

'Getting it?' I said. 'What do you mean?'

'Well, it's supposed to be funny,' said Mim, weighing the book in her hand. 'But I haven't felt like laughing once. Not even a smile.' She frowned. 'Maybe I'm just not in the mood.' And she glanced over at her tray of medicine bottles.

'Hey, Mim!' I put my hand on her shoulder. 'Not to worry!'

Mim looked back at me. 'What do you mean, not to worry?'

'I mean, not to worry. You're going to get a funny book.'

'Oh?' said Mim.

'A very funny book.'

'That's good!' Mim smiled.

'I am going to get it for you.'

'Better and better!' Mim was beginning to laugh now. 'So where is this very funny book coming from?'

'I'm going to write it.'

Mim stopped laughing.

'OK, Ed,' said Gary. 'Made up some good jokes? Got some crackers, have you?' We were at our usual place near the railings.

'Well, I thought of one.' Ed looked modest. '*How did the boy get to Oxford*?'

'Hmmm,' I said, thinking.

There was a short silence.

'OK,' said Gary. 'Let's have it.'

'*By reading!*' cried Ed.

We stared at him.

'Hey, it even works! said Ed. 'You *can* get to Oxford by reading. They're on the same rail line.'

Suddenly I clicked. 'Oh, you mean *Reading*!' I said.

'For your information,' said Gary, 'Reading is pronounced "redding", not "reading".'

'Oh.' Ed's face fell. 'That rather wrecks the joke, doesn't it?'

'Just a bit.'

Gary put his hands on his hips. 'Any others?' he asked. 'Any jokes about...Basingstoke, say?'

Ed looked uncomfortable. 'Not really.'

'What do you mean, not really?' said Gary.

'Well...it's harder to make up jokes than you think. I spent ages trying to do one about shampoo.'

'Rude, was it?' said Gary, grinning.

'No.' Ed looked surprised. 'Why should it be rude?'

'Never mind, Ed,' said Gary.

'And then I tried one about a vertical take-off hot dog.' He frowned. 'It was nearly very funny.'

'You don't say,' said Gary.

There was a short silence.

'I'll keep going,' said Ed.

'You do that, Ed,' said Gary.

The bell rang for end of break.

'Hey, Gary,' said Ed, as we made our way back to our classroom. '*Did you hear about that silly twerp who goes round saying "No"?*'

'No,' said Gary.

'Ah!' said Ed. '*It must be you, then!*'

You had to laugh...

Mim was sitting bright eyed in her chair when I got back that evening. 'Hello there!'

'Hi, Mim!'

'I've been thinking about your joke book,' she said.

'Oh, yes?' I said.

'I think it's a great idea.'

'Good.'

'To make people laugh – that is something special.'

'Yes,' I said. 'If we can.'

'Of course you can!' Mim pulled her cardigan tighter round her shoulders. 'I've been trying to think of some jokes, but do you know, I can hardly think of one.'

I looked at her sternly. 'So I got it from you, did I?'

'Got what?'

'A blank mind when it comes to jokes. I obviously got it from you. Thanks a bunch!'

Mim laughed. 'Ah, but I reckon you got your sense of humour from me. And, if you did, you're a very lucky boy!'

It was my turn to laugh.

'Oh…' Now Mim looked serious. 'We must never forget how to laugh.'

'Not likely!' I said. I mean my teachers would probably say I did a sight too much laughing.

Mim looked towards her old family photographs on the wall. 'After all, sometimes, when things are really bad…laughter is all we have.'

I didn't say anything. There have been some very sad events in our family history.

Suddenly she sat back in her chair, and crossed her arms over her chest expectantly. 'So tell me some!'

'Some what?'

'Some jokes, of course! Some of the ones you're going to put in the book'

'OK. Here's one we *might* put in. *What's a good way of stopping your eyes getting sore?*'

Her own eyes twinkled. 'Go on, I'm no good at guessing. Tell me.'

'*Take your spoon out of your coffee before you drink it,*' I said.

Miriam put back her head, and laughed until there were tears in her eyes.

'So do you think that's a good one?' I said hopefully.

'Good?' she said. 'Good? I think it's absolutely terrible!'

Chapter Three

How do aliens count up to 32?
On their fingers.

'I brought these,' Gary said next day, hauling a clutch of books from his school bag. 'Some of them are mine. And some I raided from AJ's room.' AJ (Andrew James) was Gary's little brother.

We looked at them.

Joke books.

Books of jokes.

Books of jokes that someone had collected *because they were funny.*

Our hearts rose.

Then Gary piled them on the wall, and started reading the jokes.

Our hearts sank.

They were awful. Terrible. *Lame-arama.*

They were worse than the sort you get in crackers.

These were the sort of thing – *Why is history the sweetest lesson? Because it's full of dates.* And, *What tuba can't you play? A tuba toothpaste. Why is the letter 'E' lazy? Because it's always in bed. What did Mrs Curtain call her daughter? Annette.* I mean… sad or what?

I would be worried about AJ if I was Gary, I thought. Reading too much of that sort of thing could rot your mind.

'*What song was sung when the yacht exploded?*' said Gary, turning a page. '*Pop Goes the Wee Sail.*'

We looked at each other.

'Well, it's not the way he tells 'em,' I said.

'No one could make that lot funny,' said Gary.

'They wouldn't make a dog laugh,' I said.

'I know someone whose dog laughed when he fell off his bike,' said Ed.

Gary shook his head. 'Animals don't laugh. Only humans.'

'Bats laugh, too,' said Ed. 'It's just that you can't hear them.'

'Well, how do you know they laugh?' I said.

'You can't hear them laugh because it's too high. You need a bat detector.'

Gary laughed. 'Bats detector, more like, Ed – and you'd be off the scale. Way off.'

'Oh, you think you're so—'

'Hold it, guys!' I said. Now we had the joke book to do, I didn't want to waste time fighting. 'We've got work to do.' I gestured towards the pile of books. 'There must be one halfway decent joke book there.'

Gary pulled one out. 'Here's one called *The Elephant Joke Book.*'

'It's a silly name,' said Ed. 'With that title you'd expect every single joke to be about elephants.'

'Every single joke is about elephants,' said Gary.

'Oh,' said Ed.

'Well, there must be *one* good joke about elephants in it,' I said.

'OK. Let's try and find it,' said Gary. *'What do you give a nervous elephant? Trunkquillisers.'*

We shook our heads. 'Nah!'

'What do you give a seasick elephant? Lots of room.'

I quite liked that one, actually, but the others didn't.

Gary handed the book to Ed, and asked him to find some.

Ed read out, '*What did Tarzan say when he saw the elephants coming?*'

'*Here come the elephants!*' said a voice.

We turned.

It was Rosie, the new girl.

'What did you say?' said Gary coldly.

'I said, *Here come the elephants!*'

'Why?' said Gary.

'That's the answer to the joke, isn't it?'

Ed consulted the book. 'Er...yes.'

'Hey!' Rosie grinned. 'It's nice to find people here telling jokes. I love jokes.'

We looked back at her delighted face.

'We aren't telling jokes for fun,' said Gary sternly.

'No,' I said.

'It's absolutely no fun at all,' said Ed.

There was silence. The delighted look on Rosie's face melted away. And she started backing off. '*Right...OK...*' Suddenly she thought of something. 'Oh, yes, I nearly forgot.' She held out something to Gary. It was a book – a cheery sort of book. And it was called *The Tots Fun-Time Book*.

Gary looked at it. 'Not mine.'

'I think so,' said Rosie.

'Definitely not mine,' said Gary.

'I saw you drop it,' said Rosie.

'Saw *me* drop it?' said Gary.

'Saw you drop it.'

There was a short silence.

'Maybe it got in with the others,' said Gary.

'Maybe it did,' said Rosie. And suddenly *The Tots Fun-Time Book* was in Gary's hand, and Rosie was gone.

'Well, that was definitely the biggest laugh all break!' I said.

'What was?' said Gary.

'*The Tots Fun-Time Book*.'

'It was AJ's,' said Gary.

'I know that. You know that. Rosie probably thinks it's the sort of book we read all the time.'

Gary frowned. 'I think from now on we'd better meet outside school to talk about this.'

I looked at him. 'Where?'

'Well, my place, for starters.'

Chapter Four

What do you call a donkey with three legs?
A wonkey.

I rang the bell at Gary's house, and stood in the porch, waiting.

While I was waiting I tucked the back of my shirt into my trousers.

The fact was that I didn't like going to Gary's house.

It was beautiful, with pink carpets and flowers everywhere, and everything spotless. But there was always this...atmosphere. And his mum was terrifying – there was no other word for it. I preferred going to Ed's shabby flat, with his vague, untidy dad.

'Are your parents in?' I hissed as Gary opened the door.

'Mum is. Dad's probably at his pad.' I could never understand what was going on with Gary's parents. One minute his dad was at home, stalking about grim faced, and the next he was living in the flat above his office. And before you knew it, he was back again...

I scooted upstairs, and along to his room, which had a United scarf hanging across the door.

'Who's there?' Mrs Davies called up the stairs.

'It's only Julian, Mum!' Gary called back. And he followed me in. Ed was already there, sitting on the floor, playing with a computer game. Gary always had the latest in computer games.

Gary shut the door behind him.

'OK, guys,' he said. 'Down to work.' He handed one of the books to Ed. 'You take this one, Ed. It says it's side-splitting.'

'I don't get this "side-splitting",' said Ed. 'I don't want my sides to split.'

So we started a proper trawl through Gary's and AJ's joke books.

But the jokes seemed no better than they had at school.

We argued. I voted down the chicken in the minefield (*What goes peck, peck, peck, bang?*) on the basis that everyone would have heard it at least five times before.

And Gary gave the thumbs down to, *Man: please call your dog off. Girl: I don't want to call him off. I like calling him Rover.* (Well, I thought it was funny.)

Then Ed read out, '*What do you call elves that slurp their food? Goblins.*' Gary said it was a hopeless joke, as slurping was quite different from gobbling, and he got out a packet of biscuits to demonstrate.

'That's not slurping,' said Ed, listening.

'*Is* slurping!' said Gary, through biscuit.

'You can't slurp biscuits, ' I said. 'Biscuits aren't slurpable. You can only slurp things like soup. Or gravy. Or possibly jelly, if it's not set too hard.'

Gary went on chomping.

'It's wolfing,' said Ed. 'That's what he's doing – wolfing!'

'No, I'll show you wolfing!' I grabbed a handful of biscuits, and started cramming them into my mouth.

Gary and Ed watched me, and one of them said,

'Hey, I think we're back with gobbling.' Suddenly I was laughing and spraying crumbs everywhere. And then the door opened.

It was Gary's mum. Of course. She was carrying a tray with slices of cake and drinks.

She took one look at us stuffing biscuits – and hit the roof. 'Gareth, you know you're not supposed to take food without asking!'

Gary shrugged. 'Yeah, Mum, I know. Sorry.'

'I brought you up some chocolate cake, and now you won't be hungry!' She shot me a look. I must have looked quite a sight under all those biscuit crumbs.

'It's OK, Mum!' said Gary. 'The biscuits were just for gob – I mean, for research. We were doing research for our book.'

She rolled her eyes.

Gary turned to us. 'We'll still be hungry, won't we, guys!'

'Sure!' Ed raised a hand. 'I'm always hungry.'

'Me too,' I said weakly.

Mrs Davies's face cleared a bit, and she put the tray on the floor, and went out.

'Help yourself!' said Gary.

I reached for a piece of cake when suddenly I

had a dark feeling in my stomach. Mim always used to love making cakes but lately she hadn't been up to it. I loved chocolate cake but I really didn't feel like eating any now.

'So what's with your mum?' I asked, picking at the icing.

Gary sighed. 'My dad, mainly, I reckon.'

'Nice cake,' said Ed. 'Good and sticky.'

'They just can't get on at all. It get on my nerves sometimes,' said Gary. 'And it's not good for AJ, poor little guy.'

'Yeah,' I said slowly. 'It must be hard.'

'Don't you want your cake?' said Ed.

I gave it to him gratefully. And while he munched, we went back to our joke books.

I flipped over the pages, feeling thoughtful. (That's what reading a lot of unfunny jokes can do to you.)

'What *makes* a joke funny?' I said.

'Dunno!' Ed looked at me brightly. 'What *does* make a joke funny?'

I kicked him on the thigh. 'It's not a joke, you idiot. It's a question!'

'A very *good* question too,' said Gary, in a smarmy voice.

31

'Oh, shut up, the pair of you,' I said.

Then Ed said, '*What's yellow, and points north?*'

'What?' I said with a sigh.

'*A magnetic banana.*'

Hey, we laughed.

'The 1st Pendlesham Brownies sent that one in,' said Ed.

Gary stuck his thumb up. 'Good on the 1st Pendlesham Brownies!'

But we only got about ten jokes from the joke books.

Gary put them on to his computer, and they didn't look very many at all.

He opened a new file, and turned to us. 'OK, then, ideas for out-sourcing!'

'Ideas for what?' I said.

'Out-sourcing!'

'He means finding jokes from different places,' said Ed.

'Well, I wish he'd speak English,' I grumbled.

'OK, OK!' Gary was working at the keyboard.

'What have you put down?' I asked.

Gary peered at his screen in a pleased way. 'A rather unusual border.'

'Well, stop messing!' I said. 'And get thinking...'

There was silence as we thought.

'We could ask people, of course,' said Ed.

'Get them to tell us their best jokes,' I said.

'OK. One. Asking people,' Gary typed out. 'Except I bet some people wouldn't tell us.' His face darkened. 'Some of the girls in our class are so mean.'

Ed leant forward, a gleam in the eye. 'Perhaps we could *torture* them into telling their best jokes.'

'Hmm…' said Gary. 'Do you think we'd get away with it?'

'Gary!' Ed rolled his eyes. 'It was a *joke*.'

Gary turned on him. 'This is no joking matter!' he said. 'No jokes – see?'

'But I thought—'

'Crackers!' I said quickly.

'Who, me?' said Gary.

'Yes!' said Ed.

'No, you idiots! *Crackers!* What you pull!'

And light dawned.

'Yes.' Gary nodded. 'They have jokes in.'

'They do,' said Ed.

'But not good ones,' said Gary.

'Very, very bad ones,' said Ed.

'Scrub the crackers,' ordered Gary.

'OK, then, what about libraries?' said Ed. 'Some of them have joke books.'

'Do they?' said Gary. '*Libraries?*'

'Yeah. I reckon they think if kids won't read anything else, they might read jokes.'

'Hmmm, reluctant readers. That could be quite a sales point,' said Gary. And he typed, 'Two. Libraries.'

There was silence as we went on thinking.

Then Gary said, 'There's the Internet, of course.'

'You can do that one,' I said.

'And there's Ceefax. In fact we could go down and try it now,' said Gary. 'My own telly doesn't have it.'

'Why don't you do it later, after we've gone.' I didn't want to risk another encounter with his mum.

Suddenly Gary had another idea. 'You know something, we mustn't forget comics either. Like the *Beany*. That has jokes in it.'

'Oh, yeah!' I said. 'There was a copy at our doctor's and that had some. Quite good ones.'

Ed nodded. 'Readers send them in.'

'They win bike helmets and stuff,' I said.

'When are you next going to be ill?' said Gary.

'That's no good,' I said. 'The doctor's only has one or two. What we need is a load of back copies to go though.'

'Yeah,' said Gary. 'But who on earth would collect back copies of the *Beany*?'

I shook my head. 'Who on earth?'

We looked at each other. Surely no one we knew would be so sad as to collect back copies of the *Beany*?

And then Ed gave a little cough.

Chapter Five

Little Alfie bought an ice lolly in the school tuckshop. Before he could finish it, the bell went. Not wanting to waste his lolly, he put it in his trouser pocket. The next lesson was geography.

'What do you call people who live in Asia?' asked the teacher.

'Asians,' said a little boy.

'And what about people who live in Africa?'

'Africans,' said a little girl.

'Now, Alfie,' said the teacher. 'Can you tell me what you call people who live in Europe?'

'Um...no,' said Alfie.

'European!' shouted a voice from the back.

'No, I'm not!' cried Alfie indignantly. 'My ice lolly's melting!'

'Wow, Ed, you've got zillions!'

We were in Ed's room, staring at the huge piles of *Beanies*, which he had hauled out from under his bed.

'Yup!' Ed looked at them. 'About six years there. I never threw one away.'

'A complete set.' Gary whistled.

'A slice of history,' said Ed proudly.

'A slice of something,' I said.

We stared at the stacks of comics, and then Gary reached down, and took a big chunk. 'OK, guys, let's get cracking!'

'Hey, keep them in order!' said Ed, alarmed.

'Yeah, yeah, we'll keep them in order.' Gary winked at me. 'Wouldn't dream of upsetting the archive.'

We flicked through each *Beany* to find the jokes pages, and tried them out on each other.

Some got grins.

Some got groans.

Very, very few got laughs.

One that did get a laugh was, '*What do you do if you see a space man? Park your car, man.*'

Gary and I laughed *once*. But Ed couldn't get over it, he thought it was so funny.

Gary and I found one or two quite good ones. But after a bit we drifted off the jokes pages, and started reading the cartoon-strips. Then Gary got all pompous, saying that the *Beany* had gone off since 'his day'.

We were arguing about it when Ed said, 'What do you do if you see an orange man?'

We looked at him.

'Eat it up, man!' he said, grinning. 'Good, isn't it? I made it up!'

'Yeah, yeah,' said Gary.

Finally we had each finished our pile.

We all liked, *Why did that man hit you on the head with a rolled-up comic? Oh, he's the Beany editor (head-hitter).*

In fact Gary liked it so much that he rolled up a comic and hit Ed.

'Hey!' said Ed. 'Don't do that!'

'It's OK,' said Gary. 'I'm the Ed-hitter.'

'It's not *me* I'm worried about!' said Ed, 'You just take care of my *Beanies*!'

'Well, we still haven't finished,' said Gary, looking at the pile of unread *Beanies*.

'Maybe we can finish it at the weekend,' said Ed.

'Not me!' I said. 'We're going to a wedding. My cousin Rachel is getting married.'

'Hmmm.' Gary looked thoughtful. 'They make jokes at weddings, don't they?'

'Not at the ceremony!' said Ed, sounding shocked.

'No, not at the actual *service*,' said Gary. 'But what about the reception afterwards?' He looked at me. 'Will there be any jokes made then?'

'A hundred and twenty of our lot at a party? Jokes? I think so…'

'Better take a notebook, then,' said Gary.

'Oh, sure, Gary!' I said. 'And just how—?'

'Hey, guys!' said Ed.

We looked at him.

'What do you do if you see a pink man?' said Ed.

Gary and I looked at each other.

'Pick it, man!' said Ed.

Gary and I looked at each other again.

And then suddenly we were falling over ourselves with laughter.

OK, maybe it wasn't that funny.

But it was *very* Ed.

And somehow that made it funnier than any of those other jokes.

There we were, Gary and I, rolling around the floor.

We couldn't help it. And as we laughed, I realised something. It's people who can really make you laugh – in the same way as it's people who can really make you cry…

Chapter Six

That girl looks like Helen Green.
She looks even worse in red.

Mum was standing in front of the hall mirror, putting on lipstick.

I was in a new suit and a good mood. *'Why did the woman put lipstick on her forehead? Because she wanted to make up her mind!* Duh-dah!'

Mum was hardly listening. But Dad laughed as he came downstairs. 'Better than some of your jokes, Julian,' he said. 'Not that that would be difficult!'

I had to agree.

'It's something they don't tell you about parenthood, the jokes.' mused Dad. 'I was warned about the nights and the expense and the worry and the teens. But no one ever took me aside and warned me about a deluge of terrible jokes.'

'Oh, well!' said Mum lightly. 'At least he's talking to us.'

'There is that, I suppose.' Dad looked at his watch. 'It's nearly three. We'd better get going.'

Mum put her lipstick in her black patent bag, and snapped the clasp shut. 'Hop upstairs, Julian, and see how Mim's getting on.'

I ran up, and knocked at Mim's door.

'Come in!' she called.

I went in. She was standing by the mantelpiece, wearing a dark green dress. And the jade brooch that she always wore for best. 'You look great, Mim!' I said.

And funnily enough, she did. It suited her being thinner, and her face was pale, but somehow… glowing.

She looked pleased.

'Thank you, darling.'

'I am glad you're coming.'

She laughed. 'I always was coming! It takes more

44

than my boring old illness to stop me coming to a family wedding, I can tell you!'

She walked over and put her hands on my shoulders. 'And you – Julian Lewis – you look… wonderful! So grown up in that suit! Whatever's happened to my baby?'

I laughed. 'Come on, Mim. It'll take more than a new suit to stop you treating me like your baby.'

'Well, maybe,' she agreed with a smile.

'Got everything?' I said.

She thought. 'Oh, I must take one of my new handkerchiefs, mustn't I?' I got one from the box I had given her for her birthday. It was just after we had heard that the cancer had gone to her lungs. The handkerchiefs were white and lacy and expensive. (I wasn't quite sure if she really liked them, but she put up a good show.)

As she was tucking it into her cuff, Dad called from downstairs. 'Come on, Mother. I think we should get started!'

'Coming!' Mim called back. She gave me her stick to carry, then put her arm though mine with a flourish. 'Let's be off and have us some fun!'

*

Well, I did take a notebook to the wedding. A nice new empty notebook. And I came away with a nice new empty notebook.

My main memory of the service was of cousin Rachel. I always thought her a bit of a dumpling, looks-wise. But, under the canopy with her new husband, she just glowed.

And then there was the party afterwards.

That, on the face of it, should have been a good source for jokes.

After all, there was plenty of laughing.

But it wasn't.

For none of the funny things people said or did were things you could put in a joke book. What I discovered was this. When people are really happy and pleased to see each other and have something to celebrate, they don't make *joke book* jokes. They have private jokes and family jokes, and things that make them laugh that aren't really jokes at all. Or there are jokes you can't even describe in words. The funniest thing all evening was my cousin Michael doing an imitation of Auntie Sadie inspecting the wedding presents. I laughed so much I ended up splurting a whole mouthful of Coke down my shirt front.

46

Actually I was pleased I didn't have to write down jokes – walking around with a notebook looking a complete nerd (Great idea, Gary…not!)

Everyone made a fuss of Mim. Her cough didn't seem too bad, either. She held her white lace handkerchief, but I never saw her having a really bad go. I wasn't with her much, as I thought she ought to talk to people she rarely saw. But she still managed to introduce me to one or two girls. 'Julian is writing a book,' she would say, a gleam in her eye, as she waved us away.

The first was Sarah Dines, who was related to the groom. She was wearing a pink fluffy top, which at first (but not for long) I felt like stroking.

Sarah was not impressed by my book. She just went on and on about her brother at university who had written a computer book 'with over 600 pages, not counting the index.'

'It must,' I said, 'be very thick.'

'Yes,' she said. 'It is thick.'

'Ah!' I said. 'But will it make people laugh?'

She looked shocked. 'Certainly not! It's not supposed to.'

I shook my head. 'Six hundred pages, not counting the index…and not one single joke…'

She gave a snort. She obviously thought I was a total clown. 'What's that on your shirt front?' She was looking at the Coke stain now.

'It's decoration,' I said. 'It's the latest thing. I'll do it for you, if you like.'

Sarah tossed her head. 'No, thank you.'

'Suit yourself.'

'I will. I'm going over to look at the food.'

'You do that.'

And she was gone.

But a perky girl called Tamsin *was* impressed. 'Ooh, you are clever!' she cried. ' I want to write a book!'

'What sort of book?' I said.

'Well, I've got my plot sorted out.' Tamsin confided. 'But I haven't decided whether it's going to be very sad or very funny.'

'Actually, books can be both,' I said.

Tamsin frowned. 'Sounds tricky to me. I think I'll go for just funny.' She looked at me. 'Is your book going to be funny?'

'I hope so,' I said. 'It's a joke book.'

'Oh, you're writing a joke book! That's so cool!'

'Yeah, well.' I shrugged.

'How are you finding the jokes? Do you make them up?'

I wasn't going to let on I had just been trawling though six years' worth of the *Beany*.

'Well, yes,' I said. 'We make up some of them.'

'Oh, how clever of you!' she squealed. 'Tell me one you made up.'

I looked at her big brown admiring eyes, and swallowed.

Then I caught sight of Sarah Dines, in her pink fluffy top, carrying a big plate of food. *'What is pink and fluffy?'* I said.

Tamsin grinned. 'Go on, tell me!'

I was going to say *'Sarah Dines'*, but suddenly I had this flash of complete brilliance (well I thought it was, anyway). *'Pink fluff!'* I cried.

'Pink fluff?' said Tamsin, frowning.

I nodded. 'Pink fluff.'

She thought a bit. And then she said, 'That has to be the most ridiculous joke I've ever heard!' And she pealed with laughter.

Chapter Seven

What do you call a snowman in a desert?
A puddle.

The hunt for jokes was on.

We had a book to write.

There was no slacking for Mim either. That's what I told her. She had to ring up her friends and pick their brains. When she pointed out that her friends didn't really go in for joke book type jokes, I said that was absolutely no excuse.

'Did I hear you being rather stern with Mim just now?' said Mum one evening.

'Nothing she can't take!' I said cheerfully. 'Don't worry – Mim can stick up for herself.'

'I second that,' said Dad.

We had split up Gary's 'Out-sourcing' list, and I got the library.

I didn't waste time.

'The library?' said Mum, clearing away the breakfast plates on Saturday morning.

'Yup!' I said. 'I've got to do some research.'

'Hear that, Simon?' Mum nudged Dad's shoulder (he was trying to read the business pages). 'He's off to the library. Doing research!'

'Oh, yes?' said Dad dryly. 'What sort of research would that be? Quantum theory? The history of western philosophy?'

'Um…jokes, actually.' I said.

'Ah,' said Dad.

'And what's wrong with jokes?' said Mum. 'Some jokes are highly…intellectual.'

Dad laughed.

'So what's so funny?' said Mum.

'Nothing, my love,' said Dad, turning the page.

'At least he's not on a street corner,' muttered Mum, banging shut the dishwasher. 'Quantum theory, indeed!'

52

Dad looked at me. 'I'd walk down with you, Julian, but I have to make some calls.'

'Yeah, Dad,' I said. 'You make your calls. And if you run out of things to say, ask them for their best jokes.' I nudged his shoulder. 'Clean ones, mind.'

'Cheeky monkey,' said Dad, turning another page.

As I left the kitchen, they both shouted in stereo, 'Take care at the crossing!' *The crossing?* Am I two years old? My parents!

The central library wasn't far from our house. It was a big old redbrick building. I connected it with Mim. I reckon Mum or Dad must have taken me once or twice, but not often, because they were always working so hard. Mim took me a lot when I was little. She really loved the library. I mean, If I had some time off school because there was an election or something, she would say, 'Great, we can go to…*the library*!' And she would only be half joking.

I walked in, and looked around.

And realised I was at a complete loss.

Jokes? Joke books? Humour? Well, were they fiction or non-fiction? Where did jokes come in the famous Dewey Decimal System? Presumably old Dewey had had a laugh occasionally. Well, where

did he put the funny books?

I started working along the non-fiction shelves. But the funny books were not by synchronised swimming; they were not by daily life in ancient Greece; and they were nowhere near the book on how to keep rats. I realised I wasn't going to find any joke books on my own. I needed some help.

I looked towards the desk.

The librarian, a middle-aged woman in glasses, was doing something to a pile of books. I walked slowly up to the desk. Suddenly I felt a bit unsure. *Did* libraries have joke books? Perhaps Ed had got it wrong? Or perhaps it was a joke on *me*? Maybe the middle-aged librarian would look aghast ('Jokes? Here? This is a public library, young man!'), and the two girls looking at ballet books nearby would start giggling?

The librarian looked up, and smiled. 'Can I help you?'

'Do you…?' I said. 'Er, do you have any joke books?'

'We do indeed!' she said. 'I'll show you where to find them.' And, slipping off her chair, she led me along to a shelf. It was next door to poetry. So *that's* where jokes were.

Love poems beside limericks.

54

Haikus beside howlers.

Willy Makit beside William Shakespeare...

The shelf was a low one, so I had to get down on my knees. There were nine joke books, three of which were the same as Gary's. I took all the other six over to a table.

Then I opened my notebook, took the top off my ballpoint pen, and got down to work.

The first fifteen minutes was quite fun.

The second fifteen minutes was OK.

The third fifteen minutes I was struggling a bit.

And from then on I felt I was *drowning* in jokes.

My head was awhirl with elephants in minis, and flies in soup, and chickens crossing roads, and people saying 'knock, knock'. And what ghosts eat, and what aliens think, and what doctors say to their patients, and what pupils say to their teachers. And 'What do you call a – ', 'What happens when you cross a – ', 'How can you tell if – '

I mean, after a bit I couldn't even judge whether anything was funny. It was a bit like that time we bought perfume for Mim. After the girl had squirted four different types on my wrist, I couldn't take in any more. Mum called it 'scent fatigue'. Only this time it was 'joke fatigue'.

At the beginning I had happily written down as a dead cert, *What howls at the moon in frilly knickers? An underwear-wolf.* Now I was staring at the jokes as though they were written in a foreign language. I mean, take this one – *What do you do if you see a blue banana? Cheer it up.* Was this:

    a) not funny

    b) quite funny

    c) very funny

    d) the funniest joke in the whole world?

I was still wondering when I became aware someone was standing at the table.

I looked up. It was the librarian. 'I found some more out the back,' she said, holding out a couple more joke books. It was nice of her. She clearly took pride in her job. She wasn't having me go round complaining about the lack of joke books at the central library. Oh, no!

I took them as if they were red hot.

About ten minutes later, just as I was about to pack it in, she appeared at my table again.

Not *more* joke books?

I sighed and looked up at her.

But it wasn't the librarian.

Chapter Eight

What do you call a boomerang that won't come back?
A stick.

Standing at my desk was Rosie.

Rosie from school.

Rosie in my class.

What was she doing in my library?

'What are you doing in my library?' I said.

Rosie's eyes danced. 'I'm sorry!' she cried. 'I didn't realise it was *your* library. I thought it was a public library!'

Oof!

'Of course it's a public library!' I said. 'I'm just surprised to see you here, that's all.'

'I come quite a lot,' said Rosie airily. 'I've been sitting here some time actually.' She smiled suddenly – a rather nice smile. 'I've been drawing.'

'Drawing?'

'Yes.' She put a piece of paper in front of me. 'Recognise anyone?'

I looked down at the drawing.

I did recognise someone.

It was me. It was me, poring over a lot of books with titles like *Laugh a Minute* and *The Funniest Jokes Ever* and *The Best Of British Humour*. But the expression on my face was not amused. Not amused one little bit. In fact my face was as black as thunder.

I stared at the picture.

And had three thoughts.

> 1. How dare she?
>
> 2. Rosie was really good at drawing.
>
> 3. That picture was probably the funniest thing I had encountered all morning…

I gave Rosie's picture of me to Mim.

I thought it might amuse her.

She needed cheering up, because some new pills

58

weren't working properly (I had overheard Mum and Dad talking).

'Guess who this is?' I said, as I handed her the picture.

She took it, and smiled. Then she looked at it more closely, and the smile faded.

'Hmm,' she said. 'Well, it's you, all right. Quite clearly. But not the way I like to see you.'

I laughed. ' But that's the joke, you see – me looking fed up, with all those humorous books around!'

'The joke, I get,' said Mim. 'But you don't look so much fed up to me, as…sad.'

'Oh! Do I?' I said. Then I added, quietly. 'Well, I am sometimes.'

Mim looked at me. 'I'm sorry.'

I shrugged. 'Well, you know…' I took my hand out to take the picture, but Mim held on to it. 'No, it's your present to me,' she said firmly. 'And I'm going to keep it.'

'OK,' I said.

'So tell me about this morning,' said Mim.

And I told her about the 'joke fatigue.'

'Bored with jokes, already, are you?' asked Mim.

I sighed. 'Well, those jokes I read this morning. For a start, lots of them were the same. Ed should

59

never have worried about copying from books. The people who write joke books clearly copy from each other like old monks. Sometimes if they're feeling really inventive, they'll change a name.'

Mim laughed.

'And another thing. If you really thought about them, they were virtually all…well, playing with words.'

Mim nodded. 'Wordplay. Puns.'

I frowned. 'I mean, not all jokes are like that, are they?'

'No…' Mim was thinking. 'But most children's jokes are. Children love to play with words.'

'And adults don't?'

Mim started coughing then, and I went and got her a glass of water.

She sipped it, and after a few seconds, went on with the conversation as if nothing had happened. 'Well, they do. But I think they prefer humour which comes from the way people are. Like in books, and good sit-coms.'

I nodded. 'That occurred to me once at Gary's. But when I asked what made a joke funny, they just kicked me.' I was beginning to feel rather sorry for myself.

'Did they?'

I thought for a moment. 'No, actually, come to think of it, I kicked Ed.'

'Well, that's a bit different,' said Mim.

'Anyway,' I said hastily. 'I want an example of a joke for kids that is funny without wordplay.'

'Hmm,' said Mim, thoughtfully.

'Famous Lewis blank mind, is it?'

'No,' said Mim.

'Want a bit longer to think?'

'No,' said Mim.

'You don't say you've got one?'

Mim turned to me, a look of pure triumph on her face. 'Yes! I'll see if I can remember it. It's about football.'

'Football?'

'Yes. This project of yours is getting me into areas I never dreamt of.'

'Sure is.'

'OK, then. Help me out if I need it. Two school football teams were to play each other in the final of the local…'

'Cup?' I suggested.

Mim nodded. 'That's it. One head teacher said that for every goal his team scored he would let

61

them off one evening's homework. The other head teacher said that he would give five minutes' extra break for each goal scored.'

She paused.

'And?' I prompted.

'The team captains shook hands, had a few words, and threw the coin.'

'Tossed.'

'Yes.'

'Then what?'

'At half time the score was 72–70.'

We laughed.

Chapter Nine

Boy: Where are you going?
Mother: To the doctor's. I don't like
the look of your sister.
Boy: I'll come with you. I don't
like the look of her either.

That thing with the O'Brien boys was not good.

In fact it nearly put me off the whole idea of jokes for ever – let alone writing a book of the things.

And it was all Ed's fault. Well, that's to say it was all because of the books he bought at the car boot sale.

He bought three for ten pence each, and we

thought they were the best thirty pence worth ever…

One was called *The Great Book of American Jokes*, one had golfing jokes, and one was called *The Irish Joke Book*.

Gary was particularly pleased with *The Great Book of American Jokes*. 'Excellent!' he said. 'We'll put some American jokes in. Can't afford to ignore the American market.'

'Come on, Gary!' I said, half laughing. 'You can't be serious.'

'I am!' he said. 'I've got a penfriend in Pennsylvania.' He frowned. 'Well, I wrote him a postcard three years ago anyway. Maybe he can be our agent over there. Bound to have an e-mail address now.'

'But will Americans want to buy an English joke book?'

'Of course!' said Gary. 'British humour is famous the world over – didn't you know?'

'I thought it was our teeth,' said Ed.

Gary was flipping through the book. 'Ah,' he said, 'Here's one we can use. *What do catchers eat dinner from? Home plate.*'

 'Well, I hope that gets them rolling about in

Pennsylvania,' I said. 'It doesn't do much for me.'

'Well, you're not American, are you?' said Gary. Then he paused. 'What's a sasquatch?'

'Oh, I know that,' said Ed. 'It's what Americans call a marrow. And they call aubergines eggplant,' he added helpfully.

Gary frowned. 'But it doesn't make sense.'

'Well, you're not American, are you?' I said.

Gary ignored me. 'Look, it goes, *Why does a sasquatch make a good salesman? Answer – he can easily get his foot in the door.* Well, a marrow doesn't put a foot in the door, does it?'

'Well, not in England,' I said.

Gary frowned again. 'I'm going to look it up,' he said.

I got to go off with *The Irish Joke Book.* And some of the Irish jokes were really quite good. In fact they were so good, I started telling them in the playground at break.

I didn't mean to be rude about the Irish. The jokes were just funny, that's all. They really made people laugh. It's funny to hear about people doing and saying stupid things, it just *is.* So lots of people were gathering around, and laughing their heads off…

I felt pretty good, I really did. Making people

laugh gives you a great feeling.

Making someone cry? That's easy – anyone can do it.

Make them laugh? Now that is something. That is power.

Hey, I thought, I can do this. I can really do it. Maybe I could be a stand-up when I grow up.

And then it happened. I'd just done *How do you sink an Irish submarine? Knock on the door*, and *How do you make an Irishman laugh on New Year's Day? Tell him a joke at Christmas.* Then I went on to the one about two Irishmen looking for a job, who saw an ad saying Tree Fellers wanted.

Well, I gave it my best Irish accent – *'Now look at that. Sure it's a pity there's only two of us!'* – when I saw something that made my heart lurch.

It was Barry and Dan O'Brien. And they weren't laughing. Well, they wouldn't be laughing, would they? They were Irish…

'Say that again,' said Barry quietly.

'Er…well…'

'Go on, say it again.'

'Or we'll make you,' said Dan.

 'Hey!' I said, trying to shrug it off. 'It was just a stupid joke, that's all!'

'Stupid joke!' repeated Barry.

'Yeah,' I said.

'Making us look stupid!' said Dan.

'No!' I said.

'That's what I think about your stupid jokes!' spat Barry. And he stepped forward, and threw a punch at my head.

It was a good punch, and I wasn't prepared for it. (I am not a great fighter, as my friends would be the first to agree). Caught off balance, I fell back and sideways to the ground. I scrambled quickly to my feet, just in case Barry or Dan were going to try any kicking, but Barry was standing, waiting, fists clenched.

'Come on, then!' said Barry.

'Look, guys,' I started. 'There's no—'

And then I felt another punch to my head...

'Well, Julian,' said Mrs Galbraith. 'Do you think the Irish are stupid?'

I gulped. *What sort of question was that?*

Barry and I had been hauled into the head's office. We stood side by side on the dark red carpet in front of her dark wooden desk.

Barry had already been told off for punching me.

67

But I was the one who was feeling most uncomfortable.

This was *no* joke.

'Well?' said Mrs Galbraith. 'Do you think the Irish are stupid?'

'No,' I muttered. 'Of course not.' Barry was in the same year as me, and I knew that he was really hot at maths.

'Well, why the jokes, then?'

'They're just *jokes*!' I said desperately. 'Something to laugh at! They don't mean anything.'

'Not mean anything?' Mrs Galbraith pursed her lips. 'I must say, I find that hard to believe, coming from an intelligent boy like you.' She was silent for a moment. Then she spoke quietly. 'There's a word for targeting a particular ethnic group, isn't there, Julian?'

'Yes,' I said.

'And what is that word, Julian?'

I gulped. 'Racism?'

She nodded, unsmiling. 'Yes, racism.' Suddenly she leant forward towards me. 'Now understand this, for once and for all. I won't tolerate racism in my school, in any form whatsoever!'

 I looked at her.

And she looked at me.

'Well, is that clear?' she said.

'Yes,' I said.

'Right!' She glanced over at Barry. 'You can both go back to your classrooms now.'

We walked out. Left together.

'Phew!' said Barry.

'Yeah!' I agreed.

Our eyes met for a second. And it was as good as saying sorry really…

'OK, then,' Gary said. 'No Irish jokes.'

Ed nodded. 'No Irish jokes.'

It was lunchbreak, and we'd gone outside even though it was spitting with rain. My legs were still wobbly from my mauling from Mrs G.

'Better stick to jokes about elephants,' said Gary. 'At least they don't come and thump you in the playground.'

I nodded.

'And I've been thinking,' said Gary. 'I don't think we should use any dirty jokes, either.'

I nodded again. 'Yes, those could cause trouble too. Better keep it clean.'

'Nothing rude.'

'Nothing sick,' I said.

'What's sick?' said Ed.

'I'll show you after school lunch if you like, Ed,' I said.

'No, I want to know.'

'You don't want to know, Ed,' I said kindly.

'I do. I'd just like to know what a sick joke is.'

'OK,' said Gary, and he told him a sick – a very sick – joke.

Ed's eyes popped.

'Well?' said Gary.

Ed shook his head. 'You, Gary, have a very very very sad mind.'

Then I saw Rosie. She was on her own, leaning against the wall of the PE block. She was sketching something at the end of the playground. Really concentrating. She didn't flick her eyes sideways at us, as some of the girls might have done. She was drawing as if nothing else mattered in the whole world…

Chapter Ten

Patient: Doctor, I've swallowed a fish bone!
Doctor: Are you choking?
Patient: No, I'm serious!

When I got back from school two days later I knew there was something wrong straight away. The front door was open, and Mum was standing in the hall. She was holding her mobile phone, looking worried. 'Oh, Julian, there you are. I've been waiting for you.'

'What is it?' I said. 'Is it Mim?'

'Yes!' said Mum. 'She had to go into hospital suddenly. She's taken a sudden turn for the worse, and they've had to take her in.'

My gut seemed to spasm. 'Is it serious?' I said.

Mum frowned. 'I don't really know,' she said. Mum looked me in the eye. 'She's not at all well, though. You know that, don't you?'

'Yuh,' I muttered. 'I know.'

Mum came over and put an arm round me. 'I'm sorry,' she said quietly.

I nodded. I didn't trust myself to speak. Silently I traced the pattern on the carpet with my foot. It was something I had done as a little kid, when I was waiting by the front door. Suddenly I really wanted to see my grandmother. 'Can I go?' I said.

Mum looked at me. 'Where?' she said.

'To the hospital, of course. To see Mim.'

Mum ran a hand through her hair. 'No, love, I really don't think you should. Let her rest. And Dad will report back soon. He'll be talking to the doctors.'

So that was that. I had to accept it. The grown ups had sorted everything out, as usual. I slung my school bag over my shoulder again, and started walking up the stairs.

'Got any homework?' Mum called up after me.

'Not so you'd notice,' I said.

'Oh,' said Mum. 'Well, you've got your

computer games, haven't you?' And she started flicking through her address book.

Thanks a lot, Mum, I thought furiously. Thanks for the tip – *not*! As if computer games would cheer me up! I stamped up to my room, threw my school bag on the floor, and flumped on the bed.

I didn't hear Mum when she called the first time. Then she called again, louder. 'Someone on the phone for you!'

'Oh. Ah. OK.'

I stumbled down again, picked up the receiver, still in a slight haze.

It was Gary. His voice came over loud and confident. 'Jules, hi. Gary here. Look, I think we should wrap.'

'Um…well…'

'What do you think?'

'I'm not sure I feel up to rapping,' I said.

'Sure you do!' said Gary. 'We need to wrap this joke book now – finish it off!'

'Oh, *the joke book*,' I said.

'Yes! Of course! What did you think I meant?'

'Um…I'm not sure,' I said.

'Well, anyway, we've got more than enough jokes. We ought to put the book to bed now.'

I didn't say much.

I didn't say anything about Mim.

Partly because I didn't want to make Gary feel bad. And partly because I didn't quite trust myself to speak...

But Gary didn't notice anything. He went blithely on.

'So could you and Ed meet at my place for a wrap meeting?' he said.

'Yes...if you think so,' I said.

'Well, what about tonight? Ed can make it.'

'*Tonight?*' I said.

'Yup! My parents are going out. Birthday dinner for Mum. At a French restaurant.'

'Sounds good,' I said. 'But things are a bit all over the place here. Let me think a minute!'

'OK, do you want to ring me back?'

'Yes.'

I put down the receiver, and walked into the kitchen. Mum was still on her mobile, talking to someone at work. 'Look, I'm sorry about the meeting, but I had no choice. My mother-in-law...' She glanced at me, and waved towards the teapot.

I poured out a cup, added a spoon of sugar, and  walked slowly with it up to my room.

Should I go to Gary's? I was in two minds, I really was. I mean, how could I *think* about jokes when Miriam was ill in hospital? When…when, face it, she might never come back? On the other hand, there was nothing I could *do*, stuck at home. And Mum would get any news to me at Gary's very quickly. I just didn't know what to do.

I walked into my room, and took my first sip of tea. The spoon was in it, and I got it nowhere near my eye (I leave that sort of thing to Ed!). But suddenly I thought of the joke I told Miriam the first time we talked about the book. It was such a stupid joke. But it had made her laugh.

And I made my decision.

Chapter Eleven

Father: Well, Penelope, did you get the best marks in your class this term?

Penelope: No, Daddy. Did you get the best salary in your office?

'The purpose of this meeting,' said Gary, 'is—'

'Purple!' said Ed.

Gary turned to him crossly. 'What?'

'Purple, purple, purple!'

'What?'

'I'm code-cracking!' Ed had the kids' section of the *Daily World* open, and was furiously writing down the side of a page. 'It's in code, see!'

'What's in code, Ed?' I asked.

'This joke, of course! It's written in symbols, because it's in their Junior Club section. I bet it's a *really good* joke because it's in code, see? And –' his voice rose – 'I'm cracking it. Starting with the "e"s, of course. And I'm nearly there!'

So we waited.

'I've got the whole question now!' cried Ed in triumph.

'What is it?' said Gary.

'What is purple and 4,000 miles long?'

'Hmm. So what's the answer?' said Gary.

'Nearly there! Won't take me long!' Ed was feverishly writing.

Suddenly he stopped. 'Oh,' he said.

There was silence.

'OK, then,' said Gary. 'What *is* purple and 4,000 miles long?'

'Er…the grape wall of China,' said Ed.

'These are the jokes we've more or less chosen,' said Gary, as we sat round his computer. 'I typed them out so it would be easier to decide.'

'Hey, well done!' I said.

Gary gave his cocky head-waggle. 'I get things

done – me!'

'Yeah, OK,' I said.

'Mind you, my spell-checker wouldn't take half this stuff!' Gary shook his head. 'Doesn't seem to have a sense of humour.'

We looked at the screen, while he scrolled the pages of jokes. He *had* done a lot of work too. OK, Gary had rather taken over the whole thing. But no one could say he hadn't put in the work.

'Looks great,' I said. 'I like the different sort of letters you've used.'

'Typefaces. Yeah,' said Gary, looking at the screen. Then he turned to Ed. 'Ed?'

'Mmmm,' said Ed thoughtfully. 'It's good, yes, it's good. It's just—'

'What?' said Gary.

'Well, there's something missing. Something it needs. You can't have all these pages of writing without...' He took the mouse from Gary's hand, scrolled through a few pages. 'I know!' he said suddenly. 'I know exactly what it needs.'

'What?' said Gary and I together.

'Pictures, of course!' said Ed.

We looked at each other.

*

79

'OK,' said Gary slowly. 'So who do we know who can draw?'

It was half an hour later.

We had already decided against using computer graphics (my idea), pinching them from books (Gary's idea), or drawing them ourselves (Ed's idea).

'What about Richard Benson?' said Ed.

'Can he draw?' I asked doubtfully.

'He can run,' said Ed.

'He can run, but he can't hide,' said Gary.

'He *can't* hide and he *can't* draw,' I said.

'Well, why did someone suggest him then?' said Gary testily.

'Dunno,' said Ed.

'Jamie Bennett can draw a bit,' I suggested.

'We can't have Jamie Bennett,' Gary said.

'Why not?' I asked.

'Because he's...a pain. He'd say our jokes weren't funny.'

'No!' I cried. 'Never!'

'We can't have Jamie,' said Gary firmly. 'It just wouldn't work. He'd want everything his way.'

'No, we can't have two of those,' I muttered.

'Meaning?' said Gary.

'I think you typed those jokes out really well,' I said.

We dropped the artist question, and went back to making our final selection on the jokes.

Suddenly we heard a car draw up. We stopped talking, and listened.

'It can't be them,' said Gary. 'Not so early.'

Bang, bang. Two car doors.

Silence.

A different sort of bang. The front door.

And then a furious high voice rent the air. I knew that voice, even at that pitch. It was Gary's mum. And then Gary's dad answered, lower, but also angry. I caught a few words. More than I wanted. It was X-certificate stuff. They were clearly having a mammoth row.

Ed and I looked at each other.

Then we looked at Gary.

All Gary's confidence and cockiness seemed to have drained away.

And he dropped his head in his hands.

Chapter Twelve

What's orange and sounds like a parrot?
A carrot.

'It's the second set of lifts you take. Not the first,'
said Mum. 'Are you sure you don't want to wait while
I find a parking space?'

'No,' I said. 'I don't mind going up on my own.'

Not true. I *did* mind the thought of going into the
hospital on my own. In fact I was terrified. But I
suddenly really wanted to see Mim. See where she
was, how she looked, talk to her.

I read the signs carefully, took the right lift, and

suddenly...I was there. Street to ward in seconds. No one came up and asked me what I was doing, so I walked slowly into the middle of the room, and looked round fearfully.

And even that bit wasn't difficult. There were only six or so beds – with six or so people in them. Suddenly one of the beds – one of the people – sprang into focus. I had found her.

I went over, and stood by her bed. It had her name at the top of her headrest. She seemed to be snoozing, so I said 'Hi, Mim,' very softly. But she turned her head as soon as I spoke – and smiled. 'Julian.'

'How're you doing?'

'Oh, OK,' she said. 'OK.'

I nodded. She looked pale and thin and little in the bed, but she didn't look as bad as I had imagined.

I gave her a parcel. 'I bought you something.'

'Not soap?' said Mim, and suddenly there was a glint in her eye.

I smiled. This was a family joke. Mim's mother had always been furious whenever anyone had given her soap ('What? They think I'm dirty or something?') even if it was the finest most expensive

soap you could buy. And no one in our family since then had ever given it as a present.

'No,' I said. 'Not soap.' And I gave her two books I had bought after a lot of humming and hawing and changing my mind. You had to be careful buying books for Mim. Grab them off the shelf, and she'd either read them or already knew she didn't want to.

'Oh, thank you,' said Mim. 'I'll look forward to reading them.' She took them a little stiffly, glanced at the titles, and carefully put them on her bedside table. She pulled herself a bit further up the pillows. 'So tell me about your book? It was one of the things I was thinking about, lying here.'

'Really?'

'Yes.' She made a face. 'I thought a lot about the past, and then I thought about you, and I thought about your book.'

'Good.'

'It's really taken my mind off things sometimes.'

I smiled. OK, I hadn't been allowed in myself to see her. But I had given her something to think about.

'Well, the book's coming on,' I said. 'Though it's been a lot more work that I thought. Hammering out the jokes and so on.'

'How does it work?'

'Well, we usually agree, or we take a vote…' I said. 'But if someone is really mad for a joke, it tends to go in.'

Miriam nodded. She seemed to want me to go on talking. So I did. 'Ed liked this one that goes, *Why did the teenager cross the road? Because his parents told him not to.* Gary said that it wasn't a joke at all, and I said that it might be a joke, but if so, it was a very bad one.' I paused. 'So that one's out.'

'Ah!' Mim had winced slightly, though I didn't think it was at the joke.

'But everyone agrees on your football joke. That's definitely going in.'

There was a gleam in her eye.

'Yes,' I said. 'They were dead impressed that one came from you.'

Mim smiled.

There was silence then, and I tried to think of something else to say. It was difficult, really, in that ward. At home in Mim's room I could always think of something to talk about – I mean, I didn't even have to *think* – but here it was different.

We talked a bit about the family, but it seemed Mim already had all the news from Mum and Dad.

So after a bit I went back to the joke book.

'We've decided to add some pictures,' I said. 'Just a few. But we can't find the right person to draw them.'

Mim suddenly clutched the edge of the sheet with her hand. Then she looked at me. 'Sorry, Julian, what was that?'

'I was…saying about getting someone to do some pictures.'

There was a pause. Mim's face seemed to be working. I was worried. Maybe she was in pain. But I didn't want to over-react. She called to a nurse, who came over at once. They talked about medicines, and when Mr so-and-so would be round. I didn't listen – I didn't really think it was anything to do with me. Instead I got up and looked at the collection of photographs on Mim's bedside table. There were quite a few – Dad and Mum and me at Rachel's wedding, my two aunts smiling together (an unusual sight, that), and an old black and white one of my grandfather. There was also a wince-making school photograph of me – looking a complete twerp – against a green marbled background. And slipped in among them all was a bit of paper.

I took it out, and recognised it at once. It was Rosie's picture of me at the library. And it still made me crack a smile.

And then I stopped smiling.

Of course, I thought. *Of course.* Why ever hadn't I thought of it before?

I looked at my grandmother. The nurse had gone, and her eyes were on me. 'Sorry about that,' she said.

I mean that was *so* Mim. Apologising for being ill!

'That's OK, Mim!' I said. 'In fact you've done me a favour!'

Chapter Thirteen

What's the easiest way to see flying saucers?
Trip up a waiter.

'Rosie?' Gary's voice came over the line, puzzled.
'Did you say Rosie?'

   'Yup!' I answered.

   There was a silence, and then he said, '*Rosie?*'

   '*Yes!*' I said. Gary really was being unusually thick.

   '*No way!*'

   'Why not?'

   'You know why not!'

   'No, I don't. Why can't we have Rosie?'

   'Because she's a *girl*. And we don't want some girl

muscling in on the whole thing.'

'She won't muscle. She's not the muscling sort!'

'Look, Jules,' said Gary. '*All* girls are the muscling sort – and the sooner you learn that, the better!'

'No, she's OK,' I protested.

'Don't you see?' said Gary. 'She won't understand.'

'Understand what?'

'Well, when we're…fooling around, you know, being stupid, she'll think we're…just being stupid.'

Now who was being stupid?

If I hadn't been so annoyed, I would have laughed.

I put the phone down, biting my lip. I had to think this one through. I was glad I hadn't shown I was annoyed (which is *not* the way to handle Gary). But I wasn't going to give up so easily. Oh no.

I wanted this book to be the best! It *had* to be the best!

After all, there was Mim, lying in a hospital bed, *thinking* about it. At the beginning I had wanted to do the joke book partly to take my mind off her, but it was different now. I wanted Mim to be proud of it.

I knew the book had to be as good as possible – for me, for Mim, for all the people who were going to buy it. The jokes were good (well, OK, as good as we could make them). Now the pictures had to

be good. And I knew the person who could do it. Rosie.

There was nothing for it. I would have to go to work on Ed. I picked up the phone again.

'Rosie? Who's Rosie?'

'You've only been in the same class all term, Ed.'

'The little one with glasses?'

'No, Ed. *Rosie.*'

'What does she look like?'

'Well…brown hair…slim…wears funny T-shirts sometimes.'

'Is she good at maths?'

I sighed. 'Ed, I have no idea whether Rosie is good at maths.'

'Well, the one I'm thinking of is good at maths.'

This wasn't too good. Far from getting Ed to agree to have Rosie, we hadn't even *identified* her. 'Look, Ed,' I said. '*Rosie.* You know…brown hair…pretty.' Whoops! I thought, I've given too much away there. But Ed, being Ed, didn't pick up on it.

'Does she have the old sort of French book?' he asked.

The next day I got Ed **by** the ear (literally), and *pointed* Rosie out to him.

'Yes!' he said. 'Ow – let go! Yes, that's the one I meant – she *is* the one who's good at maths.'

'Well, we've got that straight.' I let go of his ear. 'Now, listen. I want her to do the pictures for our book.'

'OK.' said Ed.

'OK?' I said in surprise. 'Do you really mean that?'

'Sure! Rosie's all right.'

'Good!' Then my eyes narrowed. 'Now for Gazza!'

'She draws really well,' I said. 'A natural!'

Gary was silent.

'And she won't take over – we won't let her. She can't anyway, now we've finished writing the book.'

Gary was still silent.

'She's good at maths!' said Ed.

'And let's face it – shut up, Ed! – who else have we got?'

There was a long silence. Then Gary bent down and slowly retied his shoelace. Then he straightened up, and said, 'We'd have to give her a trial.'

I breathed a sigh of relief.

'Sure!' I said. 'Of course!'

Suddenly Gary's face brightened. 'Actually, she may not be such a bad idea. She's got a sense of humour, I reckon. We got talking once, and she told me she really likes jokes.'

'Yes, I remember,' I said. 'We were there too. She told *all* of us she likes jokes.'

'I'll have a word with her tomorrow,' said Gary.

'Correction,' I said. 'We'll all have a word with her tomorrow.'

Chapter Fourteen

Waiter, waiter, there's a funny film
 on my soup!
What do you expect for 50p — Star Wars?

'A joke book,' said Gary.

'A book of jokes,' said Ed.

'Written by us,' said Gary.

'That's Jules, Gary and me,' said Ed.

'But it's still a sort of secret,' said Gary.

Rosie looked at the three of us. Then she laughed. 'Sheesh!' she said. 'Some secret!'

'Well, maybe one or two people know,' said Gary hastily.

'Maybe one or two,' said Rosie, with a glint in her eye.

'What we are really on about,' said Gary quickly, 'is, will you do the pictures?'

Now she was surprised. 'The pictures?'

'It's just a few,' I said. 'Not even one each page.'

'And you could use my computer,' said Gary.

Rosie shook her head slowly. 'No,' she said. 'I don't like working on a computer. I draw with my pens.'

I looked at her. 'So you'll do it?'

'Well…I'll have to think about it.'

We glanced at each other.

It had never crossed our minds that Rosie might turn us down. Up to now it had been *us* choosing *her*.

But now it was *her* deciding whether to accept *us*.

And suddenly I really wanted her to say 'Yes'.

She frowned. 'I'd like to see the jokes first – see if it's my sort of thing.'

'OK,' said Gary. 'We'll fix something up…'

'So what time did she say she was coming?' said Ed.

Gary looked at the clock on his computer. 'Any time now.'

 'I reckon Rosie's pretty reliable,' I said.

'She'd better be,' said Gary darkly.

'She's sometimes late for Geography, isn't she?' said Ed.

'I really don't know, Ed.'

'Anyway, we're not Geography,' said Gary.

'Nor we are, Gary!' I said.

'I was just thinking about the money side…' said Gary.

'Oh?'

'What sort of cut she gets.'

'Hmm,' said Ed. 'Something tells me she's not going to be a pushover.'

'Yes,' I said. 'Something tells me that too, Ed.'

There was silence.

'I hope she won't be shocked by the bra joke,' said Ed.

'What bra joke?' I said.

'Gary's bra joke,' said Ed.

'I didn't know Gary had a bra.'

'Shut up, Jules!' said Gary.

And then the bell went.

Gary leapt up, and pounded downstairs. Me – I stayed put. So did Ed.

'Hope Mrs D doesn't eat her,' I murmured.

We heard voices coming up from the hall, and

then Rosie appeared, carrying a big red folder, followed by Gary. 'Hi, guys!' she said chirpily.

'Uh…hello, Rosie,' I said. 'Welcome to the team.'

She smiled. 'Thanks, but I'm not in the team yet.'

'You will be when you see the jokes we've collected,' Gary said.

'I'll say,' I said.

Ed frowned. 'You know, guys, I'm still not sure about the pogo stick one—'

'This joke book's going to be *way cool*!' said Gary, gripping Ed by the neck.. '*Everyone* will be talking about it. *Everyone* will be buying it. It's going to be hot!'

'Cool *and* hot,' said Rosie. 'I see.'

Gary smirked. 'Well, you know what I mean.'

I looked at him. Suddenly it occurred to me that Gary was now just as keen to have Rosie in the team as I was.

'Tell me about the jokes,' said Rosie. 'Are you having any "knock, knock!" jokes, for instance?'

'We all hate "knock, knock" jokes,' said Gary.

'So we're only having one,' I said.

'I see. How does it go?'

'*Knock, knock! Go away*!' said Ed. 'I made it up,' he added modestly.

Rosie smiled.

'She smiled!' cried Ed triumphantly.

Give me another example,' said Rosie.

'*A dyslexic man walked into a bra…*' said Ed.

There was silence.

'One of Gary's!' said Ed quickly.

'But really you have to read it,' explained Gary.

'Unless you're dyslexic,' I said.

'Especially if you're dyslexic,' said Ed.

Rosie started laughing. 'You three – I don't know! You really don't need to write a joke book!'

'What do you mean by that?' said Gary suspiciously.

'But it's a very good idea,' went on Rosie, not answering. 'And yes, I'd like to do the pictures.'

'You would?' I said.

'But there's one thing I need to know.'

'Yes?' said Gary.

'What's it in aid of?'

There was silence.

'In aid of?' said Gary, puzzled.

'Yes, what *charity* is it for?'

We just stared at her blankly.

And then I found my voice. 'It's not in aid of anything,' I said. 'It's for us.'

'Oh.' Rosie looked taken aback. 'I somehow …assumed it was for charity.'

'Well, you assumed wrong,' said Gary. 'This is by us. For us. Us as in us!' he finished.

I nodded. And then suddenly, looking at Rosie's face, I felt, well…a bit *mean*. Perhaps we should be doing it for charity. Cancer research, say. Or something to do with the environment.

Ed was looking uncomfortable too. 'Well, that's an idea…' he murmured.

'We *could* do it for charity, I suppose,' I said.

But Gary was having none of it. 'Look,' he said. 'Why should we? Why does everything have to be for charity? Just because we're kids!'

We looked at him.

'It's our idea,' he went on. 'Our project, our work. Why can't we make a bit of money without everyone saying we have to do it for charity?'

There was another silence.

I did some quick thinking.

And I made my decision.

I decided to leave it.

OK, maybe it was a cop-out. Maybe we should have done it for charity all along. But it was too late to change things now. Gary had done a lot of work,

and fighting him on this could have put the whole project at risk.

That I didn't want.

And I had good reasons.

Very good reasons…

Finally Rosie broke the silence. 'OK,' she said lightly. 'It's not for charity. I've got the point.'

'But are you still prepared to come in?' I asked.

Rosie looked at me for a moment, and then her face lit up with a smile. 'Yes.'

I felt really pleased. 'Good.'

'But.'

'But what?'

'Well, I was going to work for free if it was for something I approved of. As it's not—'

'Yes?'

Rosie gave a wicked grin. 'You lot and me are going to have to talk terms!'

Chapter Fifteen

First snake: I hope we're not poisonous.
Second snake: Why?
First snake: I've just bitten my lip.

'So how is she?' I said, as I climbed into the car.

Mum was picking me up from chess club (which I found a nice change from bad jokes – except my play that night *was* a bad joke).

Mum didn't answer as she pulled out and headed down the street.

'Tell me!' I said, a bit crossly.

Then she spoke. 'Yes, Jules, we need to talk about Mim.'

'What do you mean?' I said. 'How is she?'

Well…she's not really responding to treatment, as she should.'

'Oh.'

There was silence as I let this sink in.

'It's very difficult to tell…how things are going to go from here.' Mum sighed, and slowed at some traffic lights. 'No one can really predict. But there's one thing Mim and we seem to be agreed upon.'

'Oh, yes?' I said. 'And what's that?'

'Well, we think she ought to come home…' said Mum.

My heart leapt. 'Home?'

'Yes,' said Mum. 'Anyway for a bit. See how it goes. She'd have to have a nurse, she'd go in the spare room, I don't think that would be a problem.' She glanced sideways at me 'What do you think about having Mim home?'

I thought of Mim's room, with her books, and her family photographs on the wall, and all her other things. And I said, 'Yes, I think that would be great. It's where she should be – at home with us.'

Rosie laughed. 'You can't have that joke. It's terrible.'

'Well, it made you laugh,' said Ed.

'Only because it was so terrible.'

'Yes, but—'

'Anyway, the jokes are all decided on,' interrupted Gary. 'We can't start chopping and changing now.'

'OK, OK,' Rosie got her pens out. 'So where shall I start? What joke shall I do first? '

Gary read it out. '*Why does a sasquatch make a good salesman? He can easily get his foot in the door.*'

'Um…what's a sasquatch?' said Rosie.

'It's a marrow,' said Ed.

'It's not a marrow!' said Gary.

Rosie looked at us, a bit warily.

'I looked it up, ' said Gary. 'It's a big hairy monster. American.' He paused. 'I put that joke in for the American market.'

'I see,' said Rosie. 'Well, I think I see.'

'Of course a lot of the humour will be in the drawing itself.' Gary paused. 'We hope.'

Rosie drew a long breath. 'Right!' And she set to work.

While she was working, the door opened a crack. AJ stuck his curly head round it.

'Out, AJ!' said Ed. 'We're working.'

'I know!' said AJ. 'I bought you a joke. I heard

it today in the playground.'

'Out!' said Ed.

'Just hear my joke.'

'Out!' said Ed.

But AJ looked appealingly at Rosie, who of course came to his rescue. Girls!

'Go on, AJ. Tell us your joke,' she said.

'What did the paper say to the wool?' said AJ importantly.

'I don't know,' said Gary quickly. 'What did the paper say to the wool?'

AJ threw out an arm triumphantly. 'I've got you covered!'

We looked at him blankly.

'He means *wall*,' said Ed quietly.

'He *completely* does not understand it,' said Gary.

'He's so sweet!' cried Rosie.

AJ gave her a dazzling smile. He didn't seem to mind being called sweet at all. 'I've got another!' he chirped. 'I made this one up myself.'

'No!' said Gary.

'Go on, tell us!' said Rosie.

'Why is a caterpillar?'

As we stared at him, he supplied the answer. 'Tuna!'

'OUT!' roared Gary. And he bundled him through the door.

'Actually I quite liked that one,' said Ed.

'I think he's adorable!' said Rosie.

'Yeah, yeah,' said Gary. 'Get down to work.'

Rosie gave him a look, eyebrows raised.

'If you're ready, that is,' Gary added.

And Rosie picked up her pen.

When she had finished, we gathered round.

'Well,' she said. 'Here it is. My big hairy monster.'

'It's big,' said Ed thoughtfully.

'It's hairy,' said Gary.

'And it's a monster,' said Ed.

'*It's a star!*' I cried.

'Yes...' said Gary slowly. 'I think it is...'

Then Ed asked her to draw someone who'd had an accident. 'You see, the first man says, "Have an accident?", and the other man – the man who looks all bashed up – says, "No thanks, I've already had one."' And Ed started laughing.

Rosie watched him chortling – and smiled. 'OK,' she said. 'Man who's had an accident...' And soon we were admiring her efforts again.

'Yes,' said Gary approvingly. 'Nice black eye.'

'That sling is really quite accurate,' said Ed.

Rosie's drawings were simple, but sparky. Just right.

I was dead chuffed.

We set to work, choosing the other jokes that needed pictures. Rosie had clear ideas on what would work well.

Finally she glanced at her watch, and bundled her papers into her folder. 'I've got to get my bus.'

'I've got to go too,' I said. 'Might as well walk with you to the bus stop.'

We left the house, and walked together along the street, Rosie swinging her folder. I decided against offering to carry it.

I stepped into the road to try and cross, but Rosie grabbed my arm. 'Don't do that, Julian!' she said. 'You'll end up looking like Ed's accident.'

I stepped back.

'There's a crossing further up. Come on!'

We walked on, and suddenly Rosie spoke. 'I was so sorry to hear about your grandmother.'

'Yeah,' I said. I kicked an empty beer can into the gutter. Well, almost into the gutter.

'Ed told me about her being ill. He says she's a great character.'

A great character. I frowned, thinking. That

wasn't quite right. It made Mim sound like...like a turn on the telly. But I just went, 'Mmm.'

'It must be terrible,' said Rosie. 'I mean, you're really close, aren't you?'

I nodded. 'Yes, she's always been there, always, you know...*rooted* for me. I just can't imagine life without her, somehow.'

'No, I'm sure.'

'And it's awful seeing her ill. When there's nothing you can do...'

It was good to talk to Rosie, it really was.

But the next thing she said really surprised me.

'I felt a bit guilty. When I heard.'

'*Guilty*? What for?'

She shrugged. 'Oh, you know. That silly picture I did of you. Looking miserable in the library. If I'd known about your grandmother, I wouldn't have done it.'

'Oh, that!' I said. 'Oh, don't worry about that. In fact I showed it to Mim, and we had a bit of a laugh.' I smiled. 'It was a great picture.'

Her face lit up. 'Thanks.'

We walked on in silence.

'Funny, really,' I said, after a bit.

'What's funny?'

'Seeing you in the library.'

She smiled. 'Your library.'

I put a hand on her shoulder, and stopped her walking.

'Rosie?' I said.

'Yes?'

'You are definitely allowed in my library any time you want.'

She laughed, and we went on walking. 'I was there a lot at that time, actually.'

'Really?'

'Yes.' Rosie sighed. 'We'd just moved here, and didn't know anyone and Dad was working weekends. So there wasn't much to do.'

'What about shopping?' I said.

'What about shopping? said Rosie.

I left it at that.

But she got me thinking. Perhaps life *hadn't* been so easy for Rosie recently. It couldn't be much fun, I thought, moving away from your home and friends to a new city and a new school (and let's face it, our school isn't the friendliest of places).

Rosie interrupted my thoughts. 'In fact I was quite pleased to do this joke book.'

'Were you?'

'Yes. Even though I suspected you three were nothing but trouble.'

'Us? Trouble?'

'That's what I thought. But I don't think that any longer.'

'Ah.'

'Now I *know* you're trouble.' Rosie stopped at the pelican crossing, and stabbed the button with her finger. 'But I decided I could cope with it.'

'Yes,' I said. 'I think you're doing very well.'

'And I think I'll enjoy illustrating your silly jokes.'

I squawked in half-pretend annoyance. 'Silly jokes? *Silly jokes?* I'll have you know our jokes are hand-picked height-of-cool up-to-the-minute—'

'—silly jokes,' Rosie finished for me.

'Oh, all right – silly jokes!' I agreed.

Before I could say anything else, the green man flashed, and we had to start crossing the road. 'You have to walk like him!' Rosie announced.

'Like who?' I asked.

'Like the green man,' said Rosie, pointing at the flashing panel. 'Look at the way he's drawn. He's walking with dead straight legs.'

'So he is!' I said.

'So we have to do the same.'

'OK,' I said.

I don't know what the people waiting in the cars must have thought. We must have looked pretty funny. But together we lurched across the road with dead straight legs.

It was strange, really. Sometimes just fooling around with your mates feels better than the best jokes.

Hang on a second. Mates? Rosie?

'It's good to have you back, Mim,' I said.

She smiled at me from her bed. 'Thanks. They were kind to me in the hospital, but it's much nicer here.'

'Yes,' I said.

'In fact when I got back, I felt like crying.'

'No crying allowed here, Mim,' I said sternly. 'Only laughing.'

Chapter Sixteen

A musician carrying two big bags of telephones was stopped at Customs in New York and asked what they were for.

'I don't know,' he said. 'I've just got a job with a jazz band here, and they asked me to bring two sacks of phones with me.'

I picked some flowers for Mim the day after her return. They were from the garden, yellow with lots of leaves. Only thing was they did droop rather. And the petals fell off. But she seemed quite pleased with them.

It was good to have her back. It was a strain for

Mum, I knew that, with all the different nurses and stuff, but it was the best thing for Mim. She needed to be with her family.

Over the last few weeks, her world became smaller. Soon it was just the four walls of her room. But she still got out of it sometimes. Through reading and tapes and the newspaper. And looking at the drawings for a lot of very silly jokes...

We still had more work to do at Gary's.

One Saturday Rosie and I arrived at his door at exactly the same time. I was pleased to see her. Hey, safety in numbers!

'Ready to brave the Holy Terror?' I asked, as she rang the bell.

Rosie laughed. 'Yes, Gary can be a pain, can't he?'

'No, I mean—' I broke off. Was she making a joke, or was she being serious? I was still wondering when the Holy Terror herself answered the door.

Mrs Davies stood there. Smiling. Relaxed. A different person. 'Julian! And Rosie too!' she said. 'Come on in, do. Gareth said you were coming.' She waved a hand. 'You go on up. I'll bring up some goodies in a minute.'

'Thanks, Mrs Davies,' said Rosie.

And we scooted upstairs.

AJ was sitting at the top of the stairs. He'd obviously been waiting for Rosie. 'I've got a new joke!' he said.

'Oh, yes!' said Rosie. 'What is it?'

AJ frowned, and drew a breath. 'What's the difference between a smartly dressed man and a dog in summer?'

Rosie smiled. 'Tell me.'

AJ beamed. 'One wears a suit, the other is panting!' Suddenly AJ's face fell. 'Oh no, that last bit's wrong!'

'Never mind,' said Rosie kindly. 'You tell me when you get it right.'

We went on into Gary's room. Ed was already there.

'What's up with your mum?' I said, when we had closed the door. 'She was great. I mean…you know.'

'Yeah.' Gary nodded. He looked at Rosie, and was obviously wondering whether to talk in front of her. Then he went ahead. 'Fact is, my parents have finally decided to split. Properly. Getting a divorce.'

Rosie gave a gasp. 'Oh,' she said. 'I'm sorry.'

'Nothing to be sorry about!' said Gary cheerfully. 'It's good.'

'Good?' I said.

'Sure! We all know where we are now. My parents. AJ. Me. Everyone. It's really cleared the air.'

'Yes…' I said slowly.

'It was all that coming and going I couldn't stand,' said Gary.

I could see what he was getting at. OK, so his parents were splitting. But at least now there was some certainty about things.

'So that's that,' said Gary. 'And now we can get down to work.'

I sat on his bed, thinking. Yes, I *was* pleased for Gary. Now at least life could settle down for him and AJ. And things were looking up for Rosie too. In some ways the joke book itself had been the answer to her problems. She'd found some new friends, anyway – us!

Yes, things were sorting out for them. But it wasn't going to be like that for me. There wasn't going to be any solution to my problems. I knew that…

Suddenly there was a knock at the door.

Gary tore over, and opened it. AJ was standing there.

'What did I say about interrupting us?' snapped Gary.

'I know, I know!' said AJ quickly. 'I've just got something to tell Rosie.'

'Well?' Gary barked. 'What is it?'

'It's "just pants",' said AJ.

'Just pants?' roared Gary. 'Just pants? Get out of here, you stupid little boy!' And he slammed the door. Then he went over, and sat at his computer. 'Right, now I want to talk about this printing firm my dad uses.'

But Rosie didn't seem to be listening.

She was staring at something.

Something at the end of Gary's bedroom.

Something on the floor.

I followed her gaze.

It was really quite extraordinary.

There they were. Four of Gary's thick football socks were standing on his carpet. It looked as if he had half taken them off, and then stood them up, toes up, to make strange sort of turrets. It was a really weird sight. Like a science fiction landscape.

'What are *those* doing?' said Rosie.

'Ah, yes,' said Gary. 'Effective, aren't they?'

'But what are they?' said Rosie.

Gary looked modest. 'It's a new art form I've invented.'

'A new *art form*?' said Rosie.

'Yes.' Gary looked fondly over at his socks. 'I called it Sock Art.'

'*Sock Art?*' I could see Rosie was trying hard not to burst into giggles. She looked at me helplessly, eyebrows raised. I knew what she was saying – *Is this a joke? Or is he serious?*

I looked back at her – and shrugged.

The fact was I just couldn't tell. Sometimes you couldn't with Gary…

Chapter Seventeen

What word is always pronounced wrong?
Answer: wrong.

They were strange days, Mim's last days. I couldn't really think about anything else. It was a time of dark, sickening sadness. But there were happy moments too. Such as when I read out loud to her. She liked to hear the classics, particularly Dickens, but we explored new authors too. Sometimes we put on a tape, and both of us, she in her bed, me on my chair, would listen to it. But it was a strange period in the house. Nurses and doctors coming

and going, visits by relations and friends, lots of flowers, lots of cards, lots of telephone calls. Rachel came round once, and I had a feeling she told Mim she was having a baby.

One Sunday morning, Dad came into my room. He looked drawn and grey. 'Mim wants to see you,' he said. He hesitated, and was about to say something, but then he didn't.

I went down to her room. I was used to its slightly strange – but not unpleasant – smell now. I wasn't sure, but I thought it must be something to do with her painkillers.

The nurse we had that week – a pretty blonde one – smiled, and went out of the room when I came in. Mim was lying in bed. When she saw me, she slowly put out a hand, and took mine. She looked into my face. 'It's all right,' she said. 'It's all right, Julian.'

Her eyes were untroubled. She meant it.

Everything was all right. That was what she was saying. Or that's what she wanted me to believe. But then Mim had always protected me against things – big dogs, lorries thundering too close to the pavement, Ben Brice's 'slasher' video party. She had always protected me against things, ever since I was

tiny. And now, even though she was dying, she was still doing it.

I felt a tear well up in the corner of my eye. And my picture of Mim was suddenly very clear. I smiled a wobbly smile at her. 'Is there anything you want? Can I read to you?'

She shook her head. 'No, nothing.'

She let go my hand, and we just sat there together for a few minutes.

Then she said something I couldn't catch.

'What, Mim?' I said. 'I didn't hear.'

'How about the joke book?' she whispered.

'The joke book?' I said. We hadn't talked about it for days now.

She nodded again.

'It's finished,' I said. 'It's gone to the printers.'

She nodded, happy. 'You always did manage to get things done. When you put your mind to it.' And she added, almost to herself, 'You'll be all right.'

'Rosie did a really good design for the cover,' I said.

She nodded again. 'What did you call it in the end?' (There had been a raging debate about this, all four of us wanting something different.)

'We finally went for *What's the Joke?*' I told her.

Mim nodded. '*What's the Joke?*' she repeated to herself. '*What's the Joke?*'

I mean, it was just so *weird*. My grandmother was dying, and there we were, talking about a joke book. Jokes at a time like this?

Mim must have guessed what I was thinking, because she gave a faint smile. And then suddenly I was thinking of her words that day, the one when I had first told her about the joke book. 'Sometimes, when things are really bad, it's all we have…'

It was me this time who glanced at the old picture on the wall, the photograph of Mim's father and uncle in their black clothes.

Then I took her hand again.

We looked at each other.

We didn't laugh.

But we certainly smiled…

Chapter Eighteen

What is the beginning of eternity,
The end of time and space,
The beginning of every end
And the end of every race?

Answer: the letter 'e'.

Mim died the next day. She was only sixty-six. OK, I
know people die younger than that – much younger
– but I still felt the unfairness of it. And I grieved for
her...

She never saw the finished joke book. But I
will always be grateful to it for the pleasure it gave

her in those last months. At the beginning I was doing it for me, but it helped take Mim's mind off things too, and gave her a few laughs along the way.

It must have been about ten days after the funeral that Gary rang. It was half-term. 'Hey, Jules, man!' he cried.

'Hello, Gary,' I said.

'You OK?' he said.

'Yeah. Not too bad.'

'We've got them!'

I knew at once what he meant. 'You have?'

'Yes, we've just picked them up. And the cover looks great!'

We had finally agreed to use Mr Davies's printers – not least because they did a very good deal for us. (I think it may have been Gary's dad making up for the divorce.) They were to do the stapling, a laminated cover, and everything. Everyone was relieved that Ed wasn't going to be let loose with one of those giant staplers.

'Where are you?' I said.

'In the car. The others are here too. We're picking you up at the crossroads. In about ten minutes.'

'What? You're – when…?'

124

'Picking you up. At the crossroads. In about ten minutes!'

'Hang on, hang on!'

'Can you come?'

'Well, yes, I suppose so. But which crossroads!'

'Your crossroads, you doof! The one at the bottom of your street.'

'Oh! OK!' I said. 'I'll be there!'

'You better had!' said Gary.

I looked around, found my jacket, and then went out into the evening. The sky was pale, washed looking, as if after a storm. I walked on down the street, past the familiar front doors of my childhood.

Suddenly I thought of 'door colours', a game which Mim and I had sometimes played when I was tiny. I think it must have been to help me walk when my little fat legs were getting tired. It was not exactly a demanding game. We both chose colours, and then scored a point if we walked past a house with a front door that colour. Sometimes we even chose two colours each, to increase the chances of a 'hit'.

I seemed to remember two things about the game.

One was, that I just about always had white as one of my colours.

The other was, that I just about always won.

It wasn't really surprising, I thought now, as I walked on down the curved street. After all, every second door seemed to be white...

Suddenly I saw it. Gary's dad's car was already there, waiting just past the crossroads. I walked faster. I could see Gary in the passenger seat, waving something bright orange out of the window. Rosie was in the back, and behind her, I could see Ed's unmistakable head.

I quickened my step even more. I was nearly running now. As I got closer, Rosie opened a back door, and I scrambled in.

Gary passed me back the orange book. 'So, what do you think?'

'It looks *great*!' I gazed at the title, at Rosie's drawing, at our names in big black letters. There it was – our joke book. All the way from that first idea of mine in the school playground, as Ed and Gary wrestled with each other. It was only a matter of weeks ago. But somehow it felt like a world away...

'Go on,' said Rosie. 'Open it.'

'Dud-dah!' said Ed.

Slowly I opened the top cover.

'It's a book!' I cried.

Everyone laughed.

'Wow!' I breathed.

'OK, huh?' said Ed.

'Your drawings have come out well, Rosie!' I said.

Rosie smiled. 'Yes. I thought so.'

I read the first joke.

It was one of Gary's.

Why is getting up in the morning like a pig's tail?
Because it's twirly.

I stared at the print. And suddenly I felt myself whirling far, far away. And from where I was, I thought how silly the joke was, how little it mattered, what a *detail* it was compared to the terrible things and the beautiful things that happen in life.

And then, all at once, I was back.

I read the joke again.

'Yeah, Gary,' I said. 'Good one to start with.'

And I laughed.

RED APPLES FROM ORCHARD BOOKS

Jiggy McCue Stories by Michael Lawrence

☐ The Poltergoose   ISBN 1 86039 836 7   £3.99
☐ The Killer Underpants   ISBN 1 84121 713 1   £3.99
☐ The Toilet of Doom   ISBN 1 84121 752 2   £3.99

Danger! by Tony Bradman

☐ Aftershock!   ISBN 1 84121 552 X   £3.99
☐ Hurricane!   ISBN 1 84121 588 0   £3.99

How To… by Thomas Rockwell

☐ How To Eat Fried Worms   ISBN 1 85213 722 3   £3.99
☐ How To Fight a Girl   ISBN 1 86039 347 0   £3.99

☐ Do Not Read This Book
    by P   ISBN 1 84121 390 2   £3.99

Red Apple books are available from all good bookshops,
or can be ordered direct from the publisher:
Orchard Books, PO BOX 29, Douglas IM99 1BQ
Credit card orders please telephone 01624 836000
or fax 01624 837033
or e-mail: bookshop@enterprise.net for details.

To order please quote title, author and ISBN
and your full name and address.
Cheques and postal orders should be made
payable to 'Bookpost plc.'
Postage and packing is FREE within the UK
(overseas customers should add £1.00 per book).

Prices and availability are subject to change.